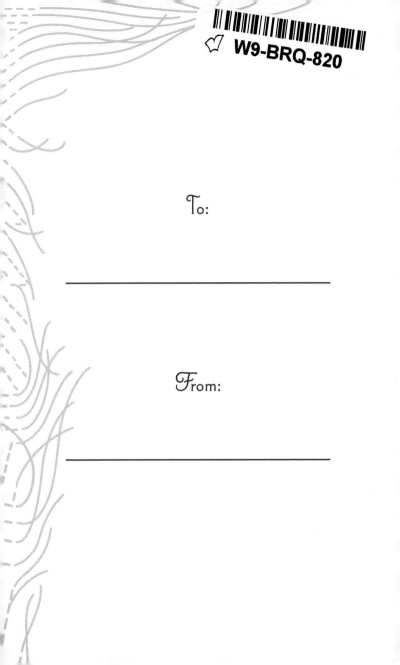

W9-BRQ-820

To:

_____

From:

_____

CHRISTMAS
with
Louisa May Alcott

CHRISTMAS

with

Louisa May Alcott

STERLING
New York

STERLING
New York

An Imprint of Sterling Publishing Co., Inc.

STERLING and the distinctive Sterling logo are registered trademarks
of Sterling Publishing Co., Inc.

Compilation and cover ©2021 Sterling Publishing Co., Inc.

ISBN 978-1-4549-4438-6

Distributed in Canada by Sterling Publishing Co., Inc.
c/o Canadian Manda Group, 664 Annette Street
Toronto, Ontario M6S 2C8, Canada
Distributed in the United Kingdom by GMC Distribution Services
Castle Place, 166 High Street, Lewes, East Sussex BN7 1XU, England
Distributed in Australia by NewSouth Books
University of New South Wales, Sydney, NSW 2052, Australia

For information about custom editions, special sales, and premium and
corporate purchases, please contact Sterling Special Sales at
800-805-5489 or specialsales@sterlingpublishing.com.

Manufactured in the United States

2 4 6 8 10 9 7 5 3

sterlingpublishing.com

Cover illustration by Yehrin Tong
Cover design by Melissa Farris
Interior design by Rich Hazelton

Contents

A Christmas Dream, and How It Came to Be True

I'm so tired of Christmas I wish there never would be another one!" exclaimed a discontented-looking little girl, as she sat idly watching her mother arrange a pile of gifts two days before they were to be given.

"Why, Effie, what a dreadful thing to say! You are as bad as old Scrooge; and I'm afraid something will happen to you, as it did to him, if you don't care for dear Christmas," answered mamma, almost dropping the silver horn she was filling with delicious candies.

"Who was Scrooge? What happened to him?" asked Effie, with a glimmer of interest in her listless face, as she picked out the sourest lemondrop she could find; for nothing sweet suited her just then.

"He was one of Dickens's best people, and you can read the charming story some day. He hated Christmas until a strange dream showed him how dear and beautiful it was, and made a better man of him."

"I shall read it; for I like dreams, and have a great many curious ones myself. But they don't keep me from being tired of Christmas," said Effie, poking discontentedly among the sweeties for something worth eating.

"Why are you tired of what should be the happiest time of all the year?" asked mamma, anxiously.

"Perhaps I shouldn't be if I had something new. But it is always the same, and there isn't any more surprise about it. I always find heaps of goodies in my stocking. Don't like some of them, and soon get tired of those I do like. We always have a great dinner, and I eat too much, and feel ill next day. Then there is a Christmas tree somewhere, with a doll on top, or a stupid old Santa

Claus, and children dancing and screaming over bonbons and toys that break, and shiny things that are of no use. Really, mamma, I've had so many Christmases all alike that I don't think I *can* bear another one." And Effie laid herself flat on the sofa, as if the mere idea was too much for her.

Her mother laughed at her despair, but was sorry to see her little girl so discontented, when she had everything to make her happy, and had known but ten Christmas days.

"Suppose we don't give you *any* presents at all,—how would that suit you?" asked mamma, anxious to please her spoiled child.

"I should like one large and splendid one, and one dear little one, to remember some very nice person by," said Effie, who was a fanciful little body, full of odd whims and notions, which her friends loved to gratify, regardless of time, trouble, or money; for she was the last of three little girls, and very dear to all the family.

"Well, my darling, I will see what I can do to please you, and not say a word until all is ready. If I could only get a new idea to start with!" And mamma went on tying up her pretty bundles with a thoughtful face, while Effie strolled to the window to watch the rain that kept her in-doors and made her dismal.

"Seems to me poor children have better times than rich ones. I can't go out, and there is a girl about my age splashing along, without any maid to fuss about rubbers and cloaks and umbrellas and colds. I wish I was a beggar-girl."

"Would you like to be hungry, cold, and ragged, to beg all day, and sleep on an ash-heap at night?" asked mamma, wondering what would come next.

"Cinderella did, and had a nice time in the end. This girl out here has a basket of scraps on her arm, and a big old shawl all round her, and doesn't seem to care a bit, though the water runs out of the toes of her boots. She goes paddling along, laughing at the rain, and eating a cold potato as if it tasted nicer than the chicken and ice-cream I had for dinner. Yes, I do think poor children are happier than rich ones."

"So do I, sometimes. At the Orphan Asylum today I saw two dozen merry little souls who have no parents, no home, and no hope of Christmas beyond a stick of candy or a cake. I wish you had been there to see how happy they were, playing with the old toys some richer children had sent them."

"You may give them all mine; I'm so tired of them I never want to see them again," said Effie, turning from the window to the pretty baby-house full of everything a child's heart could desire.

"I will, and let you begin again with something you will not tire of, if I can only find it." And mamma knit her brows trying to discover some grand surprise for this child who didn't care for Christmas.

Nothing more was said then; and wandering off to the library, Effie found "A Christmas Carol," and curling herself up in the sofa corner, read it all before tea. Some of it she did not understand; but she laughed and cried over many parts of the charming story, and felt better without knowing why.

All the evening she thought of poor Tiny Tim, Mrs. Cratchit with the pudding, and the stout old gentleman who danced so gayly that "his legs twinkled in the air." Presently bedtime arrived.

"Come, now, and toast your feet," said Effie's nurse, "while I do your pretty hair and tell stories."

"I'll have a fairy tale to-night, a very interesting one," commanded Effie, as she put on her blue silk wrapper and little fur-lined slippers to sit before the fire and have her long curls brushed.

So nurse told her best tales; and when at last the child lay down under her lace curtains, her head was full of a curious jumble of Christmas elves, poor children, snow-storms, sugarplums, and surprises. So it is no wonder that she dreamed all night; and this was the dream, which she never quite forgot.

She found herself sitting on a stone, in the middle of a great field, all alone. The snow was falling fast, a bitter wind whistled by, and night was coming on. She felt hungry, cold, and tired, and did not know where to go nor what to do.

"I wanted to be a beggar-girl, and now I am one; but I don't like it, and wish somebody would come and take care of me. I don't know who I am, and I think I must be lost," thought Effie, with the curious interest one takes in one's self in dreams. But the more she thought about it, the more bewildered she felt. Faster fell the snow, colder blew the wind, darker grew the night; and poor Effie made up her mind that she was quite forgotten and left to freeze alone. The tears were chilled on her cheeks, her feet felt like icicles, and her heart died within her, so hungry, frightened, and forlorn was she. Laying her head on her knees, she gave herself up for lost, and sat there with the great flakes fast turning her to a little white mound, when suddenly the sound of music reached her, and starting up, she looked and listened with all her eyes and ears.

Far away a dim light shone, and a voice was heard singing. She tried to run toward the welcome glimmer, but could not stir, and stood like a small statue of expectation while the light drew nearer, and the sweet words of the song grew clearer.

"From our happy home
　　Through the world we roam
　One week in all the year,
　　Making winter spring
　　With the joy we bring,
　For Christmas-tide is here.

Now the eastern star
Shines from afar
To light the poorest home;
Hearts warmer grow,
Gifts freely flow,
For Christmas-tide has come.

Now gay trees rise
Before young eyes,
Abloom with tempting cheer;
Blithe voices sing,
And blithe bells ring,
For Christmas-tide is here.

Oh, happy chime,
Oh, blessed time,
That draws us all so near!
'Welcome, dear day,'
All creatures say,
For Christmas-tide is here."

A child's voice sang, a child's hand carried the
little candle; and in the circle of soft light it shed,

Effie saw a pretty child coming to her through the night and snow. A rosy, smiling creature, wrapped in white fur, with a wreath of green and scarlet holly on its shining hair, the magic candle in one hand, and the other outstretched as if to shower gifts and warmly press all other hands.

Effie forgot to speak as this bright vision came nearer, leaving no trace of footsteps in the snow, only lighting the way with its little candle, and filling the air with the music of its song.

"Dear child, you are lost, and I have come to find you," said the stranger, taking Effie's cold hands in his, with a smile like sunshine, while every holly berry glowed like a little fire.

"Do you know me?" asked Effie, feeling no fear, but a great gladness, at his coming.

"I know all children, and go to find them; for this is my holiday, and I gather them from all parts of the world to be merry with me once a year."

"Are you an angel?" asked Effie, looking for the wings.

"No; I am a Christmas spirit, and live with my mates in a pleasant place, getting ready for our holiday, when we are let out to roam about the world, helping make this a happy time for all who will let us in. Will you come and see how we work?"

"I will go anywhere with you. Don't leave me again," cried Effie, gladly.

"First I will make you comfortable. That is what we love to do. You are cold, and you shall be warm; hungry, and I will feed you; sorrowful, and I will make you gay."

With a wave of his candle all three miracles were wrought,—for the snow-flakes turned to a white fur cloak and hood on Effie's head and shoulders, a bowl of hot soup came sailing to her lips, and vanished when she had eagerly drunk the last drop; and suddenly the dismal field changed to a new world so full of wonders that all her troubles were forgotten in a minute. Bells were ringing so merrily that it was hard to keep from dancing. Green garlands hung on the walls, and every tree was a Christmas tree full of toys, and blazing with candles that never went out.

In one place many little spirits sewed like mad on warm clothes, turning off work faster than any sewing-machine ever invented, and great piles were made ready to be sent to poor people. Other busy creatures packed money into purses, and wrote checks which they sent flying away on the wind,— a lovely kind of snow-storm to fall into a world below full of poverty. Older and graver spirits were looking over piles of little books, in which the records of the past year were kept, telling how different people had spent it, and what sort of gifts they deserved. Some got peace, some disappointment, some remorse and sorrow, some great joy and hope. The rich had generous thoughts sent them; the poor, gratitude and contentment. Children had more love and duty to parents; and parents renewed patience, wisdom, and satisfaction for and in their children. No one was forgotten.

"Please tell me what splendid place this is?" asked Effie, as soon as she could collect her wits after the first look at all these astonishing things.

"This is the Christmas world; and here we work all the year round, never tired of getting ready for the happy day. See, these are the saints just setting off; for some have far to go, and the children must not be disappointed."

As he spoke the spirit pointed to four gates, out of which four great sleighs were just driving, laden with toys, while a jolly old Santa Claus sat in the middle of each, drawing on his mittens and tucking up his wraps for a long cold drive.

"Why, I thought there was only one Santa Claus, and even he was a humbug," cried Effie, astonished at the sight.

"Never give up your faith in the sweet old stories, even after you come to see that they are only the pleasant shadow of a lovely truth."

Just then the sleighs went off with a great jingling of bells and pattering of reindeer hoofs, while all the spirits gave a cheer that was heard in the lower world, where people said, "Hear the stars sing."

"I never will say there isn't any Santa Claus again. Now, show me more."

"You will like to see this place, I think, and may learn something here perhaps."

The spirit smiled as he led the way to a little door, through which Effie peeped into a world of dolls. Baby-houses were in full blast, with dolls of all sorts going on like live people. Waxen ladies sat in their parlors elegantly dressed; black dolls cooked in the kitchens; nurses walked out with the bits of dollies; and the streets were full of tin soldiers marching, wooden horses prancing, express wagons rumbling, and little men hurrying to and fro. Shops were there, and tiny people buying legs of mutton, pounds of tea, mites of clothes, and everything dolls use or wear or want.

But presently she saw that in some ways the dolls improved upon the manners and customs of human beings, and she watched eagerly to learn why they did these things. A fine Paris doll driving in her carriage took up a black worsted Dinah who was hobbling along with a basket of clean clothes, and carried her to her journey's end, as if it were the proper thing to do. Another interesting china lady took off her comfortable red cloak and put it round a poor wooden creature done up in a paper shift, and so badly painted that its face would have sent some babies into fits.

"Seems to me I once knew a rich girl who didn't give her things to poor girls. I wish I could remember who she was, and tell her to be as kind as that china doll," said Effie, much touched at the sweet way the pretty creature wrapped up the poor fright, and then ran off in her little gray gown to buy a shiny fowl stuck on a wooden platter for her invalid mother's dinner.

"We recall these things to people's minds by dreams. I think the girl you speak of won't forget this one." And the spirit smiled, as if he enjoyed some joke which she did not see.

A little bell rang as she looked, and away scampered the children into the red-and-green school-house with the roof that lifted up, so one could see how nicely they sat at their desks with mites of books, or drew on the inch-square blackboards with crumbs of chalk.

"They know their lessons very well, and are as still as mice. We make a great racket at our school, and get bad marks every day. I shall tell the girls they had better mind what they do, or their dolls will be better scholars than they are," said Effie, much impressed, as she peeped in and saw no rod in the hand of the little mistress, who looked up and shook her head at the intruder, as if begging her to go away before the order of the school was disturbed.

Effie retired at once, but could not resist one look in at the window of a fine mansion, where the family were at dinner, the children behaved so well at table, and never grumbled a bit when their mamma said they could not have any more fruit.

"Now, show me something else," she said, as they came again to the low door that led out of Doll-land.

"You have seen how we prepare for Christmas; let me show you where we love best to send our good and happy gifts," answered the spirit, giving her his hand again.

"I know. I've seen ever so many," began Effie, thinking of her own Christmases.

"No, you have never seen what I will show you. Come away, and remember what you see to-night."

Like a flash that bright world vanished, and Effie found herself in a part of the city she had never seen before. It was far away from the gayer places, where every store was brilliant with lights and full of pretty things, and every house wore a festival air, while people hurried to and fro with merry greetings. It was down among the dingy streets where the poor lived, and where there was no making ready for Christmas.

Hungry women looked in at the shabby shops, longing to buy meat and bread, but empty pockets forbade. Tipsy men drank up their wages in the bar-rooms; and in many cold dark chambers little children huddled under the thin blankets, trying to forget their misery in sleep.

No nice dinners filled the air with savory smells, no gay trees dropped toys and bonbons into eager hands, no little stockings hung in rows beside the chimney-piece ready to be filled, no happy sounds of music, gay voices, and dancing feet were heard; and there were no signs of Christmas anywhere.

"Don't they have any in this place?" asked Effie, shivering, as she held fast the spirit's hand, following where he led her.

"We come to bring it. Let me show you our best workers." And the spirit pointed to some sweet-faced men and women who came stealing into the poor houses, working such beautiful miracles that Effie could only stand and watch.

Some slipped money into the empty pockets, and sent the happy mothers to buy all the comforts they needed; others led the drunken men out of temptation, and took them home to find safer pleasures there. Fires were kindled on cold hearths, tables spread as if by magic, and warm clothes wrapped round shivering limbs. Flowers suddenly bloomed in the chambers of the sick; old people found themselves remembered; sad hearts were consoled by a tender word, and wicked ones softened by the story of Him who forgave all sin.

But the sweetest work was for the children; and Effie held her breath to watch these human fairies hang up and fill the little stockings without which a child's Christmas is not perfect, putting in things that once she would have thought very humble presents, but which now seemed beautiful and precious because these poor babies had nothing.

"That is so beautiful! I wish I could make merry Christmases as these good people do, and be loved and thanked as they are," said Effie, softly, as she watched the busy men and women do their work and steal away without thinking of any reward but their own satisfaction.

"You can if you will. I have shown you the way. Try it, and see how happy your own holiday will be hereafter."

As he spoke, the spirit seemed to put his arms about her, and vanished with a kiss.

"Oh, stay and show me more!" cried Effie, trying to hold him fast.

"Darling, wake up, and tell me why you are smiling in your sleep," said a voice in her ear; and opening her eyes, there was mamma bending over her, and morning sunshine streaming into the room.

"Are they all gone? Did you hear the bells? Wasn't it splendid?" she asked, rubbing her eyes, and looking about her for the pretty child who was so real and sweet.

"You have been dreaming at a great rate,— talking in your sleep, laughing, and clapping your hands as if you were cheering some one. Tell me what was so splendid," said mamma, smoothing the tumbled hair and lifting up the sleepy head.

Then, while she was being dressed, Effie told her dream, and Nursey thought it very wonderful; but mamma smiled to see how curiously things the child had thought, read, heard, and seen through the day were mixed up in her sleep.

"The spirit said I could work lovely miracles if I tried; but I don't know how to begin, for I have no magic candle to make feasts appear, and light up groves of Christmas trees, as he did," said Effie, sorrowfully.

"Yes, you have. We will do it! we will do it!" And clapping her hands, mamma suddenly began to dance all over the room as if she had lost her wits.

"How? how? You must tell me, mamma," cried Effie, dancing after her, and ready to believe anything possible when she remembered the adventures of the past night.

"I've got it! I've got it!—the new idea. A splendid one, if I can only carry it out!" And mamma waltzed the little girl round till her curls flew wildly in the air, while Nursey laughed as if she would die.

"Tell me! tell me!" shrieked Effie.

"No, no; it is a surprise,—a grand surprise for Christmas day!" sung mamma, evidently charmed with her happy thought. "Now, come to breakfast; for we must work like bees if we want to play spirits tomorrow. You and Nursey will go out shopping, and get heaps of things, while I arrange matters behind the scenes."

They were running downstairs as mamma spoke, and Effie called out breathlessly,—

"It won't be a surprise; for I know you are going to ask some poor children here, and have a tree or something. It won't be like my dream; for they had ever so many trees, and more children than we can find anywhere."

"There will be no tree, no party, no dinner, in this house at all, and no presents for you. Won't that be a surprise?" And mamma laughed at Effie's bewildered face.

"Do it. I shall like it, I think; and I won't ask any questions, so it will all burst upon me when the time comes," she said; and she ate her breakfast thoughtfully, for this really would be a new sort of Christmas.

All that morning Effie trotted after Nursey in and out of shops, buying dozens of barking dogs, woolly lambs, and squeaking birds; tiny tea-sets, gay picture-books, mittens and hoods, dolls and candy. Parcel after parcel was sent home; but when Effie returned she saw no trace of them, though she peeped everywhere. Nursey chuckled, but wouldn't give a hint, and went out again in the afternoon with a long list of more things to buy; while Effie wandered forlornly about the house, missing the usual merry stir that went before the Christmas dinner and the evening fun.

As for mamma, she was quite invisible all day, and came in at night so tired that she could only lie on the sofa to rest, smiling as if some very pleasant thought made her happy in spite of weariness.

"Is the surprise going on all right?" asked Effie, anxiously; for it seemed an immense time to wait till another evening came.

"Beautifully! better than I expected; for several of my good friends are helping, or I couldn't have done it as I wish. I know you will like it, dear, and long remember this new way of making Christmas merry."

Mamma gave her a very tender kiss, and Effie went to bed.

The next day was a very strange one; for when she woke there was no stocking to examine, no pile of gifts under her napkin, no one said "Merry Christmas!" to her, and the dinner was just as usual to her. Mamma vanished again, and Nurse kept wiping her eyes and saying: "The dear things! It's the prettiest idea I ever heard of. No one but your blessed ma could have done it."

"Do stop, Nursey, or I shall go crazy because I don't know the secret!" cried Effie, more than once; and she kept her eye on the clock, for at seven in the evening the surprise was to come off.

The longed-for hour arrived at last, and the child was too excited to ask questions when Nurse put on her cloak and hood, led her to the carriage, and they drove away, leaving their house the one dark and silent one in the row. "I feel like the girls in the fairy tales who are led off to strange places and see fine things," said Effie, in a whisper, as they jingled through the gay streets.

"Ah, my deary, it is like a fairy tale, I do assure you, and you will see finer things than most children will tonight. Steady, now, and do just as I tell you, and don't say one word whatever you see," answered Nurse, quite quivering with excitement as she patted a large box in her lap, and nodded and laughed with twinkling eyes.

They drove into a dark yard, and Effie was led through a back door to a little room, where Nurse coolly proceeded to take off not only her cloak and hood, but her dress and shoes also. Effie stared and bit her lips, but kept still until out of the box came a little white fur coat and boots, a wreath of holly leaves and berries, and a candle with a frill of gold paper round it. A long "Oh!" escaped her then; and when she was dressed and saw herself in the glass, she started back, exclaiming, "Why, Nursey, I look like the spirit in my dream!"

"So you do; and that's the part you are to play, my pretty! Now whist, while I blind your eyes and put you in your place."

"Shall I be afraid?" whispered Effie, full of wonder; for as they went out she heard the sound of many voices, the tramp of many feet, and, in spite of the bandage, was sure a great light shone upon her when she stopped.

"You needn't be; I shall stand close by, and your ma will be there."

After the handkerchief was tied about her eyes, Nurse led Effie up some steps, and placed her on a high platform, where something like leaves touched her head, and the soft snap of lamps seemed to fill the air. Music began as soon as Nurse clapped her hands, the voices outside sounded nearer, and the tramp was evidently coming up the stairs.

"Now, my precious, look and see how you and your dear ma have made a merry Christmas for them that needed it!"

Off went the bandage; and for a minute Effie really did think she was asleep again, for she actually stood in "a grove of Christmas trees," all gay and shining as in her vision. Twelve on a side, in two rows down the room, stood the little pines, each on its low table; and behind Effie a taller one rose to the roof, hung with wreaths of popcorn, apples, oranges, horns of candy, and cakes of all sorts, from sugary hearts to gingerbread Jumbos. On the smaller trees she saw many of her own discarded toys and those Nursey bought, as well as heaps that seemed to have rained down straight from that delightful Christmas country where she felt as if she was again.

"How splendid! Who is it for? What is that noise? Where is mamma?" cried Effie, pale with pleasure and surprise, as she stood looking down the brilliant little street from her high place.

Before Nurse could answer, the doors at the lower end flew open, and in marched twenty-four little blue-gowned orphan girls, singing sweetly, until amazement changed the song to cries of joy and wonder as the shining spectacle appeared. While they stood staring with round eyes at the wilderness of pretty things about them, mamma stepped up beside Effie, and holding her hand fast to give her courage, told the story of the dream in a few simple words, ending in this way:—

"So my little girl wanted to be a Christmas spirit too, and make this a happy day for those who had not as many pleasures and comforts as she has. She likes surprises, and we planned this for you all. She shall play the good fairy, and give each of you something from this tree, after which every one will find her own name on a small tree, and can go to enjoy it in her own way. March by, my dears, and let us fill your hands."

Nobody told them to do it, but all the hands were clapped heartily before a single child stirred; then one by one they came to look up wonderingly at the pretty giver of the feast as she leaned down to offer them great yellow oranges, red apples, bunches of grapes, bonbons, and cakes, till all were gone, and a double row of smiling faces turned toward her as the children filed back to their places in the orderly way they had been taught.

Then each was led to her own tree by the good ladies who had helped mamma with all their hearts; and the happy hubbub that arose would have satisfied even Santa Claus himself,—shrieks of joy, dances of delight, laughter and tears (for some tender little things could not bear so much pleasure at once, and sobbed with mouths full of candy and hands full of toys). How they ran to show one another the new treasures! how they peeped and tasted, pulled and pinched, until the air was full of queer noises, the floor covered with papers, and the little trees left bare of all but candles!

"I don't think heaven can be any gooder than this," sighed one small girl, as she looked about her in a blissful maze, holding her full apron with one hand, while she luxuriously carried sugar-plums to her mouth with the other.

"Is that a truly angel up there?" asked another, fascinated by the little white figure with the wreath on its shining hair, who in some mysterious way had been the cause of all this merry-making.

"I wish I dared to go and kiss her for this splendid party," said a lame child, leaning on her crutch, as she stood near the steps, wondering how it seemed to sit in a mother's lap, as Effie was doing, while she watched the happy scene before her. Effie heard her, and remembering Tiny Tim, ran down and put her arms about the pale child, kissing the wistful face, as she said sweetly, "You may; but mamma deserves the thanks. She did it all; I only dreamed about it."

Lame Katy felt as if "a truly angel" was embracing her, and could only stammer out her thanks, while the other children ran to see the pretty spirit, and touch her soft dress, until she stood in a crowd of blue gowns laughing as they held up their gifts for her to see and admire.

Mamma leaned down and whispered one word to the older girls; and suddenly they all took hands to dance round Effie, singing as they skipped.

It was a pretty sight, and the ladies found it hard to break up the happy revel; but it was late for small people, and too much fun is a mistake. So the girls fell into line, and marched before Effie and mamma again, to say goodnight with such grateful little faces that the eyes of those who looked grew dim with tears. Mamma kissed every one; and many a hungry childish heart felt as if the touch of those tender lips was their best gift. Effie shook so many small hands that her own tingled; and when Katy came she pressed a small doll into Effie's hand, whispering, "You didn't have a single present, and we had lots. Do keep that; it's the prettiest thing I got."

"I will," answered Effie, and held it fast until the last smiling face was gone, the surprise all over, and she safe in her own bed, too tired and happy for anything but sleep.

"Mamma, it *was* a beautiful surprise, and I thank you so much! I don't see how you did it; but I like it best of all the Christmases I ever had, and mean to make one every year. I had my splendid big present, and here is the dear little one to keep for love of poor Katy; so even that part of my wish came true."

And Effie fell asleep with a happy smile on her lips, her one humble gift still in her hand, and a new love for Christmas in her heart that never changed through a long life spent in doing good.

How It All Happened

It was a small room, with nothing in it but a bed, two chairs, and a big chest. A few little gowns hung on the wall, and the only picture was the wintry sky, sparkling with stars, framed by the uncurtained window. But the moon, pausing to peep, saw something pretty and heard something pleasant. Two heads in little round night-caps lay on one pillow, two pairs of wide-awake blue eyes stared up at the light, and two tongues were going like mill clappers.

"I'm so glad we got our shirts done in time! It seemed as if we never should, and I don't think six cents is half enough for a great red flannel thing with four button-holes—do you?" said one little voice, rather wearily.

"No; but then we each made four, and fifty cents is a good deal of money. Are you sorry we didn't keep our quarters for ourselves?" asked the other voice, with an under-tone of regret in it.

"Yes, I am, till I think how pleased the children will be with our tree, for they don't expect anything, and will be so surprised. I wish we had more toys to put on it, for it looks so small and mean with only three or four things."

"It won't hold any more, so I wouldn't worry about it. The toys are very red and yellow, and I guess the babies won't know how cheap they are, but like them as much as if they cost heaps of money."

This was a cheery voice, and as it spoke the four blue eyes turned toward the chest under the window, and the kind moon did her best to light up the tiny tree standing there. A very pitiful little tree it was—only a branch of hemlock in an old flower-pot, propped up with bits of coal, and hung with a few penny toys earned by the patient fingers of the elder sisters, that the little ones should not be disappointed.

But in spite of the magical moonlight the broken branch, with its scanty supply of fruit, looked pathetically poor, and one pair of eyes filled slowly with tears, while the other pair lost their happy look, as if a cloud had come over the sunshine.

"Are you crying, Dolly?"

"Not much, Polly."

"What makes you, dear?"

"I didn't know how poor we were till I saw the tree, and then I couldn't help it," sobbed the elder sister, for at twelve she already knew something of the cares of poverty, and missed the happiness that seemed to vanish out of all their lives when father died.

"It's dreadful! I never thought we'd have to earn our tree, and only be able to get a broken branch, after all, with nothing on it but three sticks of candy, two squeaking dogs, a red cow, and an ugly bird with one feather in its tail"; and overcome by a sudden sense of destitution, Polly sobbed even more despairingly than Dolly.

"Hush, dear; we must cry softly, or mother will hear, and come up, and then we shall have to tell. You know we said we wouldn't seem to mind not having any Christmas, she felt so sorry about it."

"I *must* cry, but I'll be quiet."

So the two heads went under the pillow for a few minutes, and not a sound betrayed them as the little sisters cried softly in one another's arms, lest mother should discover that they were no longer careless children, but brave young creatures trying to bear their share of the burden cheerfully.

When the shower was over, the faces came out shining like roses after rain, and the voices went on again as before.

"Don't you wish there really was a Santa Claus, who knew what we wanted, and would come and put two silver half-dollars in our stockings, so we could go and see *Puss in Boots* at the Museum to-morrow afternoon?"

"Yes, indeed; but we didn't hang up any stockings, you know, because mother had nothing to put in them. It does seem as if rich people might think of poor people now and then. Such little bits of things would make us happy, and it couldn't be much trouble to take two small girls to the play, and give them candy now and then."

"*I* shall when I'm rich, like Mr. Chrome and Miss Kent. I shall go round every Christmas with a big basket of goodies, and give *all* the poor children some."

"P'r'aps if we sew ever so many flannel shirts we may be rich by-and-by. I should give mother a new bonnet first of all, for I heard Miss Kent say no lady would wear such a shabby one. Mrs. Smith said fine bonnets didn't make real ladies. I like her best, but I do want a locket like Miss Kent's."

"I should give mother some new rubbers, and then I should buy a white apron, with frills like Miss Kent's, and bring home nice bunches of grapes and good things to eat, as Mr. Chrome does. I often smell them, but he never gives *me* any; he only says, 'Hullo, chick!' and I'd rather have oranges any time."

"It will take us a long while to get rich, I'm afraid. It makes me tired to think of it. I guess we'd better go to sleep now, dear."

"Good-night, Dolly."

"Good-night, Polly."

Two soft kisses were heard, a nestling sound followed, and presently the little sisters lay fast asleep cheek against cheek, on the pillow wet with their tears, never dreaming what was going to happen to them to-morrow.

Now Miss Kent's room was next to theirs, and as she sat sewing she could hear the children's talk, for they soon forgot to whisper. At first she smiled, then she looked sober, and when the prattle ceased she said to herself, as she glanced about her pleasant chamber:

"Poor little things! they think I'm rich, and envy me, when I'm only a milliner earning my living. I ought to have taken more notice of them, for their mother has a hard time, I fancy, but never complains. I'm sorry they heard what I said, and if I knew how to do it without offending her, I'd trim a nice bonnet for a Christmas gift, for she *is* a lady, in spite of her old clothes. I can give the children some of the things they want anyhow, and I will. The idea of those mites making a fortune out of shirts at six cents apiece!"

Miss Kent laughed at the innocent delusion, but sympathized with her little neighbors, for she knew all about hard times. She had good wages now, but spent them on herself, and liked to be fine rather than neat. Still, she was a good-hearted girl, and what she had overheard set her to thinking soberly, then to acting kindly, as we shall see.

"If I hadn't spent all my money on my dress for the party to-morrow night, I'd give each of them a half-dollar. As I can not, I'll hunt up the other things they wanted, for it's a shame they shouldn't have a bit of Christmas, when they tried so hard to please the little ones."

As she spoke she stirred about her room, and soon had a white apron, an old carnelian heart on a fresh blue ribbon, and two papers of bon-bons ready. As no stockings were hung up, she laid a clean towel on the floor before the door, and spread forth the small gifts to look their best.

Miss Kent was so busy that she did not hear a step come quietly up stairs, and Mr. Chrome, the artist, peeped at her through the balusters, wondering what she was about. He soon saw, and watched her with pleasure, thinking that she never looked prettier than now.

Presently she caught him at it, and hastened to explain, telling what she had heard, and how she was trying to atone for her past neglect of these young neighbors. Then she said good-night, and both went into their rooms, she to sleep happily, and he to smoke as usual.

But his eye kept turning to some of the "nice little bundles" that lay on his table, as if the story he had heard suggested how he might follow Miss Kent's example. I rather think he would not have disturbed himself if he had not heard the story told in such a soft voice, with a pair of bright eyes full of pity looking into his, for little girls were not particularly interesting to him, and he was usually too tired to notice the industrious creatures toiling up and down stairs on various errands, or sewing at the long red seams.

Now that he knew something of their small troubles, he felt as if it would please Miss Kent, and be a good joke, to do his share of the pretty work she had begun.

So presently he jumped up, and, opening his parcels, took out two oranges and two bunches of grapes, then he looked up two silver half-dollars, and stealing into the hall, laid the fruit upon the towel, and the money atop of the oranges. This addition improved the display very much, and Mr. Chrome was stealing back, well pleased, when his eye fell on Miss Kent's door, and he said to himself, "She too shall have a little surprise, for she is a dear, kind-hearted soul."

In his room was a prettily painted plate, and this he filled with green and purple grapes, tucked a sentimental note underneath, and leaving it on her threshold, crept away as stealthily as a burglar.

The house was very quiet when Mrs. Smith, the landlady, came up to turn off the gas. "Well, upon my word, here's fine doings, to be sure!" she said, when she saw the state of the upper hall. "Now I wouldn't have thought it of Miss Kent, she is such a giddy girl, nor of Mr. Chrome, he is so busy with his own affairs. I meant to give those children each a cake to-morrow, they are such good little things. I'll run down and get them now, as my contribution to this fine set out."

Away trotted Mrs. Smith to her pantry, and picked out a couple of tempting cakes, shaped like hearts and full of plums. There was a goodly array of pies on the shelves, and she took two of them, saying, as she climbed the stairs again, "They remembered the children, so I'll remember them, and have my share of the fun."

So up went the pies, for Mrs. Smith had not much to give, and her spirit was generous, though her pastry was not of the best. It looked very droll to see pies sitting about on the thresholds of closed doors, but the cakes were quite elegant, and filled up the corners of the towel handsomely, for the apron lay in the middle, with the oranges right and left, like two sentinels in yellow uniforms.

It was very late when the flicker of a candle came up stairs, and a pale lady, with a sweet sad face, appeared, bringing a pair of red and a pair of blue mittens for her Dolly and Polly. Poor Mrs. Blake did have a hard time, for she stood all day in a great store that she might earn bread for the poor children who staid at home and took care of one another. Her heart was very heavy that night, because it was the first Christmas she had ever known without gifts and festivity of some sort. But Petkin, the youngest child, had been ill, times were very hard, the little mouths gaped for food like the bills of hungry birds, and there was no tender mate to help fill them.

If any elves had been hovering about the dingy hall just then, they would have seen the mother's tired face brighten beautifully when she discovered the gifts, and found that her little girls had been so kindly remembered. Something more brilliant than the mock diamonds in Miss Kent's best earrings fell and glittered on the dusty floor as Mrs. Blake added the mittens to the other things, and went to her lonely room again, smiling as she thought how she could thank them all in a sweet and simple way.

Her windows were full of flowers, for the delicate tastes of the poor lady found great comfort in their beauty. "I have nothing else to give, and these will show how grateful I am," she said, as she rejoiced that the scarlet geraniums were so full of gay clusters, the white chrysanthemum stars were all out, and the pink roses at their loveliest.

They slept now, dreaming of a sunny morrow as they sat safely sheltered from the bitter cold. But that night was their last, for a gentle hand cut them all, and soon three pretty nosegays stood in a glass, waiting for dawn, to be laid at three doors, with a few grateful words which would surprise and delight the receivers, for flowers were rare in those hard-working lives, and kind deeds often come back to the givers in fairer shapes than they go.

Now one would think that there had been gifts enough, and no more could possibly arrive, since all had added his or her mite except Betsey, the maid, who was off on a holiday, and the babies fast asleep in their trundle-bed, with nothing to give but love and kisses. Nobody dreamed that the old cat would take it into her head that her kittens were in danger, because Mrs. Smith had said she thought they were nearly old enough to be given away. But she must have understood, for when all was dark and still, the anxious mother went patting up stairs to the children's door, meaning to hide her babies under their bed, sure they would save them from destruction. Mrs. Blake had shut the door, however, so poor Puss was disappointed; but finding a soft, clean spot among a variety of curious articles, she laid her kits there, and kept them warm all night, with her head pillowed on the blue mittens.

In the cold morning Dolly and Polly got up and scrambled into their clothes, not with joyful haste to see what their stockings held, for they had none, but because they had the little ones to dress while mother got the breakfast.

Dolly opened the door, and started back with a cry of astonishment at the lovely spectacle before her. The other people had taken in their gifts, so nothing destroyed the magnificent effect of the treasures so curiously collected in the night. Puss had left her kits asleep, and gone down to get her own breakfast, and there, in the middle of the ruffled apron, as if in a dainty cradle, lay the two Maltese darlings, with white bibs and boots on, and white tips to the tiny tails curled round their little noses in the sweetest way.

Polly and Dolly could only clasp their hands and look in rapturous silence for a minute; then they went down on their knees and revelled in the unexpected richness before them.

"I do believe there *is* a Santa Claus, and that he heard us, for here is everything we wanted," said Dolly, holding the carnelian heart in one hand and the plummy one in the other.

"It must have been some kind of a fairy, for we didn't mention kittens, but we wanted one, and here are two darlings," cried Polly, almost purring with delight as the downy bunches unrolled and gaped till their bits of pink tongues were visible.

"Mrs. Smith was one fairy, I guess, and Miss Kent was another, for that is her apron. I shouldn't wonder if Mr. Chrome gave us the oranges and the money: men always have lots, and his name is on this bit of paper," said Dolly.

"Oh, I'm *so* glad! Now we shall have a Christmas like other people, and I'll never say again that rich folks don't remember poor folks. Come and show all our treasures to mother and the babies; they must have some," answered Polly, feeling that the world was all right, and life not half as hard as she thought it last night.

Shrieks of delight greeted the sisters, and all that morning there was joy and feasting in Mrs. Blake's room, and in the afternoon Dolly and Polly went to the Museum, and actually saw *Puss in Boots*; for their mother insisted on their going, having discovered how the hard-earned quarters had been spent. This was such unhoped-for bliss that they could hardly believe it, and kept smiling at one another so brightly that people wondered who the happy little girls in shabby cloaks could be who clapped their new mittens so heartily, and laughed till it was better than music to hear them.

This was a very remarkable Christmas-day, and they long remembered it; for while they were absorbed in the fortunes of the Marquis of Carabas and the funny cat, who tucked his tail in his belt, washed his face so awkwardly, and didn't know how to purr, strange things were happening at home, and more surprises were in store for our little friends. You see, when people once begin to do kindnesses, it is so easy and pleasant they find it hard to leave off; and sometimes it beautifies them so that they find they love one another very much—as Mr. Chrome and Miss Kent did, though we have nothing to do with that except to tell how they made the poor little tree grow and blossom.

They were very jolly at dinner, and talked a good deal about the Blakes, who ate in their own rooms. Miss Kent told what the children said, and it touched the soft spot in all their hearts to hear about the red shirts, though they laughed at Polly's lament over the bird with only one feather in its tail.

"I'd give them a better tree if I had any place to put it, and knew how to trim it up," said Mr. Chrome, with a sudden burst of generosity, which so pleased Miss Kent that her eyes shone like Christmas candles.

"Put it in the back parlor. All the Browns are away for a week, and we'll help you trim it—won't we, my dear?" cried Mrs. Smith, warmly; for she saw that he was in a sociable mood, and thought it a pity that the Blakes should not profit by it.

"Yes, indeed; I should like it of all things, and it needn't cost much, for I have some skill in trimmings, as you know." And Miss Kent looked so gay and pretty as she spoke that Mr. Chrome made up his mind that millinery must be a delightful occupation.

"Come on then, ladies, and we'll have a little frolic. I'm a lonely old bachelor, with nowhere to go to-day, and I'd like some fun."

They had it, I assure you; for they all fell to work as busy as bees, flying and buzzing about with much laughter as they worked their pleasant miracle. Mr. Chrome acted more like the father of a large family than a crusty bachelor, Miss Kent's skillful fingers flew as they never did before, and Mrs. Smith trotted up and down as briskly as if she were sixteen instead of being a stout old woman of sixty.

The children were so full of the play, and telling all about it, that they forgot their tree till after supper; but when they went to look for it they found it gone, and in its place a great paper hand with one finger pointing down stairs, and on it these mysterious words in red ink:

"Look in the Browns' back parlor!"

At the door of that interesting apartment they found their mother with Will and Petkin, for another hand had suddenly appeared to them pointing up. The door flew open quite as if it were a fairy play, and they went in to find a pretty tree planted in a red box on the center table, lighted with candles, hung with gilded nuts, red apples, gay bonbons, and a gift for each.

Mr. Chrome was hidden behind one folding-door, and fat Mrs. Smith squeezed behind the other, and they both thought it a great improvement upon the old-fashioned Santa Claus to have Miss Kent, in the white dress she made for the party, with Mrs. Blake's roses in her hair, step forward as the children gazed in silent rapture, and with a few sweet words welcome them to the little surprise their friends had made.

There were many Christmas trees in the city that night, but none which gave such hearty pleasure as the one which so magically took the place of the broken branch and its few poor toys. They were all there, however, and Dolly and Polly were immensely pleased to see that of all her gifts Petkin chose the forlorn bird to carry to bed with her, the one yellow feather being just to her taste.

Mrs. Blake put on her neat bonnet, and was so gratified that Miss Kent thought it the most successful one she ever trimmed. She was well paid for it by the thanks of one neighbor and the admiration of another; for when she went to her party Mr. Chrome went with her, and said something on the way which made her heart dance more lightly than her feet that night.

Good Mrs. Smith felt that her house had covered itself with glory by this event, and Dolly and Polly declared that it was the most perfect and delightful surprise party ever seen.

It was all over by nine o'clock, and with good-night kisses for every one the little girls climbed up to bed laden with treasures and too happy for many words. But as they tied their round caps Dolly said, thoughtfully:

"On the whole, I think it's rather nice to be poor when people are kind to you."

"Well, I'd *rather* be rich; but if I can't be, it is very good fun to have Christmas trees like this one," answered truthful Polly, never guessing that they had planted the seed from which the little pine-tree grew so quickly and beautifully.

When the moon came to look in at the window on her nightly round, two smiling faces lay on the pillow, which was no longer wet with tears, but rather knobby with the mine of riches hidden underneath,—first fruits of the neighborly friendship which flourished in that house until another and a merrier Christmas came.

Signature Select Classics

Elegantly Designed Booklets of Poetry and Prose

This book is part of Sterling Publishing's Signature Select Classics chapbook series. Each booklet features distinguished poetry and prose by the world's greatest poets and writers in an elegantly designed and printed chapbook binding. Compact and portable, they fit comfortably in the hand and can be carried conveniently anywhere. These books are essential reading for lovers of classic literature and collectible editions in their own right. They make perfect keepsakes to own and to share with others.